MY SIDE
of the Story

Printed in the United States of America

Second Edition

10 9 8 7 6 5 4 3 2 1

Library of Congress Catalog Card Number: 2003091341

ISBN: 0-7868-3647-4

Visit www.disneybooks.com

MY SIDE
of the Story

By Cinderella

As told to Daphne Skinner
Illustrated by Atelier Philippe Harchy

Disney
PRESS

New York

1

Don't Worry; Don't Hurry

When I was a little girl and my father was still alive, he used to read me animal stories. One of my favorites was the story of the tortoise and the hare. The hare made fun of the tortoise for being slow, and challenged him to a race.

"Very well," said the tortoise, setting off at his usual unhurried pace. The hare bounded ahead. He was so sure he would win that he lay down for a nap.

When he awoke, the tortoise was crossing the finish line.

"So the tortoise won?" I asked my father.

He nodded. Then he asked, "What would you rather be, Ella, a tortoise or a hare?"

"Neither," I said. "I want to be a princess. Or a veterinarian."

This made him laugh. "Why not both?" he said.

Years later, I still treasure his words.

As for the story of the tortoise and the hare, it was the inspiration for my own personal motto, "Don't worry; don't hurry."

This was not a popular concept in my house.

Ever since my father passed away and my stepmother put me to work, my days have begun pretty much the same way—with my stepsisters screaming for me at the top of their lungs.

No matter how promptly I would bring their breakfast trays, it was never fast enough, and that morning was no exception.

"You are so slow!" Drizella whined as I set down her tray. I smiled sweetly and headed toward the door. She pointed to a pile of clothing on the floor. "Wash those things right away," she said.

Anastasia was next. The moment she saw me, she started screeching about the ironing, which was in a big basket at the foot of her bed.

"Do it now, not three days from now!" she ordered, sounding like a rusty pump handle. Her voice was sharp enough to shatter crockery.

My stepmother was last. She gave me work, too—a big bag of mending. "See that it gets done quickly," she added.

"Yes, Stepmother," I murmured.

I was just starting down the stairway when I heard a bloodcurdling scream. It was Anastasia. She hurtled out of her room. "A big, ugly mouse! Under my teacup! It got away before I could kill it!"

Whew, I thought.

My stepsisters hate mice. If they knew how many were living in the house, they'd try to kill them all.

And that would be terrible, because the mice are my very best friends.

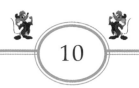

2

Mice Are Nice

I've always loved animals, perhaps because my father told me so many stories about them. Now that he's gone, they're my only friends. They're much nicer to me than my stepfamily. Bruno the dog licks my face every morning when I come down to the kitchen. The chickens cluck like cheerful old ladies when I greet them. Only Lucifer, my stepmother's cat, keeps his distance. He's as nasty as she is.

Still, it was because of Lucifer that I met the mice.

One afternoon I noticed Lucifer crouching in a corner, batting something around. It was a mouse, and the poor thing was nearly dead.

"Lucifer!" I cried. "Leave that mouse alone!"

He ran off, hissing, and I carried the mouse up to my garret. When the tiny creature's trembling stopped, I learned something amazing: if I listened very carefully, I could understand what he was saying.

It was the most wonderful thing that had ever happened to me. Then and there, my loneliness ended.

The mouse, whose name was Jaq, chattered away, and before long his little mouse family and friends—Mert, Bert, Suzy, Perla, and Luke—joined us. (Gus came later.) They were fascinating.

They knew all kinds of things about the house (it has 632 working mouse holes), the barnyard (the chickens lay more eggs when the rooster tells jokes), and my stepfamily.

I found out that Anastasia often hides sweets in her room, which the mice eat. Then Anastasia blames Drizella, and they have one of their screaming fights. The mice find this very entertaining.

Drizella has an imaginary friend named Drizoola, who she sings to.

My stepmother has dreams of becoming a great lady and yearns for the day when she and her daughters will shine at court. She cannot understand why she has never been invited to the palace. "If only they could meet us," she often says when she is alone, "they would know *at once* that we are superior people."

The mice dissolved into peals of squeaky laughter as they told me this. "We'll get to the palace faster than they will!" said Mert.

"At least we've got decent manners!" said Bert.

Their low opinion of my stepfamily should have been comforting, but talk of the palace made me sad.

"What's wrong, Cinderelly?" asked Perla.

"I know it's foolish, but ever since I was a little girl, I've dreamed of being a princess." I sighed. "The palace seems as far away as the moon."

There was a brief silence.

"Anything is possible," said Bert.

"After all, we learned how to talk," said Mert.

"And to sew," said Perla and Suzy.

"And to lift fifty times our body weight," added Jaq.

None of that will help me, I thought. How could it?

3

If . . .

It turned out it was Gus who had been under Anastasia's teacup. He told me it was Lucifer who put him on her breakfast tray.

Lucifer! I thought. What is your *problem*? I was dusting the foyer, wondering if some traumatic event in Lucifer's kittenhood was causing him to act out in such an antisocial way, when a knock at the door interrupted my thoughts.

"Open up! Royalgram!"

I opened the door to a man carrying a mailbag as big as a washtub. It was filled with envelopes bearing the royal seal.

"Urgent message from the King!" he said, handing me an envelope.

What could the King possibly want with our household? I wondered.

There was only one way to find out.

I went to the music room, where my stepsisters were practicing. Anastasia's shrill flute playing and Drizella's off-key attempts to sing along were not having a good effect on my stepmother. She looked ill.

For a moment I felt sorry for her.

Then she saw me. "Cindy!" she snapped, using the nickname I hate. "I've told you never to interrupt us during our music lessons!"

"This Royalgram just arrived from the palace," I announced.

"The PALACE?!" She snatched the envelope, ripped it open, and began to read:

"The King is giving a ball in honor of the Prince. And by Royal Command, every eligible maiden is to attend. Every eligible maiden!" She gasped, sinking into a chair.

"Eligible?" screamed my stepsisters. "That's us!"

At a palace ball, I thought, I could at least pretend I was a princess. That would be fun. "I'm an eligible maiden, too," I said.

They stared at me. "You? At the palace!" cried Drizella.

"It does say, 'Every eligible maiden is to attend,'" I pointed out.

My stepmother smiled. For a moment she looked like Lucifer when he was tormenting little Gus.

"You're right, Cindy," she said slowly. "You can go—"

My stepsisters shouted in protest.

"—*if* you get all your work done . . ."

I can do that, I thought.

". . . and *if* you can find something suitable to wear," she added. My stepsisters laughed, as if it could never happen.

But I knew better. I already had something suitable to wear.

I was going to the ball!

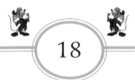

A few minutes later, I was showing the mice my dearest possession—a pink silk dress that had belonged to my mother.

"It's perfect for the ball, isn't it?" I asked.

"It *is* pretty," said Perla, cocking her head.

"But a touch old-fashioned," said Suzy.

"It has possibilities," said Jaq. "Maybe with shorter sleeves, a sash, some beads . . ."

"Makeover!" squeaked the mice, jumping up and down. "Fun!"

"Hmmm," I said. "You have a point." Just as we were trying to figure out where to find a sash, or beads, my stepmother called my name.

"I'll be back soon," I said.

How wrong I was.

A New Motto

They were all waiting for me. Smirking, Anastasia and Drizella handed me slips of paper.

One said:

Do the following for Anastasia—TODAY

1. Remove all green buttons from green dress.

2. Replace all green buttons with blue buttons.

3. Wash and dry feathers on blue headdress.

4. Darn holes in blue silk stockings.

5. Repair beading on green evening purse.

6. Steam and brush green velvet evening cape.

7. Sew torn seams in blue evening gloves.

8. Polish flute.

The second one said:

Do these things for Drizella before she goes to the ball—<u>and you don't</u>!

1. Wash yellow dress, purple dress, and red dress.
2. Iron yellow dress, purple dress, and red dress.
3. Polish orange shoes, yellow shoes, pink shoes, green shoes, white shoes, gray shoes, brown shoes, and black shoes.
4. Sew purple ribbons on green headdress.
5. Repair torn hem on evening cape.
6. Go fly a kite! Ha! Ha!

It would take me days to do all these tasks, and they knew it!

"When you've finished helping Anastasia and Drizella," said my stepmother, "you can do a few last-minute chores for me."

My heart sank right down to my feet. I tried not to cry.

"Wax the banisters," she began. "Scrub the fire screen. Clean the andirons. Give Lucifer a bath. Polish the soup tureen and the fish knives." She smiled cruelly. "*If* you get everything done," she said, "and *if* you dress suitably, you can come to the ball."

By midafternoon, I was beginning to wonder if "Don't worry; don't hurry" was truly the best motto for me. I had been working for hours, but many tasks—polishing Drizella's big, stinky shoes, and bathing my stepmother's large, nasty cat—still lay ahead.

I couldn't possibly finish in time if I kept going so slowly.

So I came to a decision.

I changed my motto.

It became: "Those who wish to complete a large amount of tasks in a short period of time must accelerate the pace of their movements."

In other words, I decided to hurry up.

Lucifer—yowling like a demon in torment—got his bath. I polished the andirons and the soup tureen.

By nightfall, I was up to the fish knives. As I was polishing the last one, I heard the sound of horses' hooves. The carriage had arrived to take us to the ball.

But how could I go? I wondered hopelessly. My dress wasn't ready.

Anastasia and Drizella clattered downstairs in their finery, followed by my stepmother.

"Why, Cindy," she observed, "you haven't finished your chores yet!"

You made sure of that, I thought. But all I said was, "I'm not going to the ball—I'm going to my room."

I ran upstairs in tears.

"Surprise!" squeaked the mice. I blinked in amazement. There on my bed lay an elegant pink gown, complete with a sash; new, extremely fashionable sleeves; and beautiful beadwork.

"We sewed it for you!" cried Perla, Suzy, Gus, and Jaq. "Do you like it?"

"It's beautiful!" I said. "Shall I put it on?"

"Yes! Yes!" they squeaked. "The coach is waiting! Hurry!"

I took their advice, and moments later I was downstairs, facing my stepfamily.

"I found something to wear!" I said breathlessly. "Is there room for me in the coach?"

Their answer came quickly, and it made me see that I had misjudged my stepsisters. I knew they were lazy, noisy, sloppy, and tone-deaf, but I had always believed that they weren't all bad.

I was so wrong!

Screaming with rage, Anastasia accused me of stealing her sash. Drizella chimed in, claiming I had taken her beads. Then they tore my gown to shreds.

I begged my stepmother to stop them, but she did nothing until my dress was in tatters. Then she said, "Come, girls. We don't want to be late," and they all left.

5

Menchika-whatta?

"You can't go to the ball looking like that. You're a mess!"

I was out in the garden, crying, and I just wanted to be alone. Go away, I thought, whoever you are.

"Now, where's my magic wand?"

That question definitely got my attention. I looked up.

A plump woman in a blue cape was standing over me, looking puzzled. A wand appeared in the air, and she grabbed it. "Gotcha!" she cried. It began to twinkle.

I sat up. "How did you *do* that?" I asked.

"Easiest Fairy Godmother trick in the book," she said.

"You mean . . . you're a Fairy Godmother?" I said in disbelief.

"Honey," she said, "I'm *your* Fairy Godmother. I'm Dorabella, vice president of Regional Makeovers, and I've come here to help you."

"Makeover! Makeover!" squeaked the mice, led by Gus and Jaq. "Fun!"

Dorabella checked her big, diamond-studded wristwatch. "We'd better hurry," she said. "It's late."

She rolled up her sleeves, pointed her wand at a big pumpkin, and began to chant. On her last words—which sounded something like "Bibbidi-Bobbidi-Boo"—the pumpkin turned into a big, shiny coach.

This made the mice squeak so hard that they bounced.

"I'll bet *you'd* like to go to the palace," said Dorabella, and they bounced even higher.

"Thought so," she said, and then things began to change very fast. Chanting and waving her wand, she turned four of the mice into coach horses, the farmyard horse into a coachman, and Bruno the dog into a footman, complete with powdered wig and buckled shoes.

I began to feel giddy.

Dorabella glanced at her watch. "Hmmm. Time flies when you're having fun," she said. "Remember that."

"I—I'll try," I replied.

"Do or don't do. There is no try," she said sternly.

What does *that* mean? I wondered, but before I could ask her, she was chanting again and waving her wand at *me*.

I couldn't believe what happened next. My hair styled itself into an intricate French twist. My rags became a shimmering ball gown with a skirt as big as a chicken coop. A pair of glass slippers appeared on my feet. Amazing!

But Dorabella was frowning at my feet. "Drat," she murmured, "just look at your feet! And there's no time for a pedicure."

I didn't care. As far as I was concerned, the makeover was perfect. "Fairy Godmother!" I cried. "How can I ever thank you?"

"Just keep track of the time, honey," she said, tapping her watch. "The makeover ends at midnight. Now jump into the coach and go have yourself a ball!"

6

Is It Midnight Already?

"Excuse me, may I have this dance?"

I whirled around in surprise. An extremely handsome young man, wearing a SAVE THE WHALES pin on his lapel, was smiling at me.

"Why, of course," I said. I had been admiring the many paintings of dogs, horses, chickens, and guinea pigs that adorned the walls.

As he led me onto the dance floor, he asked, "You like animals?"

"I love them!" I said. "I've never seen such fine portraits of chickens before."

His face lit up. "I'm going to study chickens someday," he said, "if I ever get to veterinary college."

"You want to be a vet?" I asked. "I do, too!"

He looked deep into my eyes. "I have a hunch we're the only two people here who share that dream. I'm lucky I found you."

My heart thumped. "I—I feel the same way," I said.

Still talking, we waltzed into the garden. I told him about understanding mice. He told me about whispering to horses. We discovered that we both wanted to make the world a better place for animals.

We were on a little bridge, waltzing to the music of the frogs, when he kissed me.

I have never been so happy, I thought.

And then the palace clock began to chime. It was almost midnight. The spell was about to end!

"Oh, no!" I cried and began to turn away.

"Stop!" the handsome stranger called after me. But how could I? When the clock finished striking, I would be in rags, sitting on a pumpkin.

I ran through the ballroom, ignoring the stares of the guests, and fled from the palace. My coach and horses were waiting at the foot of the stairway.

"Thank goodness!" I gasped, scrambling down the stairs so hastily that I lost one of my slippers.

I hesitated. The clock struck again.

"Hurry, Cinderella!" called the footman. "I'm growing a tail!"

I left the slipper, flung myself into the coach, and we were off.

The next morning, all I could think about was the handsome stranger.

"He's the man of my dreams," I told the chickens as I threw corn to them. "Even if I never see him again, I'll never, ever forget him."

Dorabella's spell had ended at midnight, just as she had warned. The coachman turned back into a horse. The footman turned into Bruno, and the horses into mice. My gown was gone forever.

"But I still have one glass slipper," I told the chickens, "and I'll treasure it always."

They clucked as if they understood.

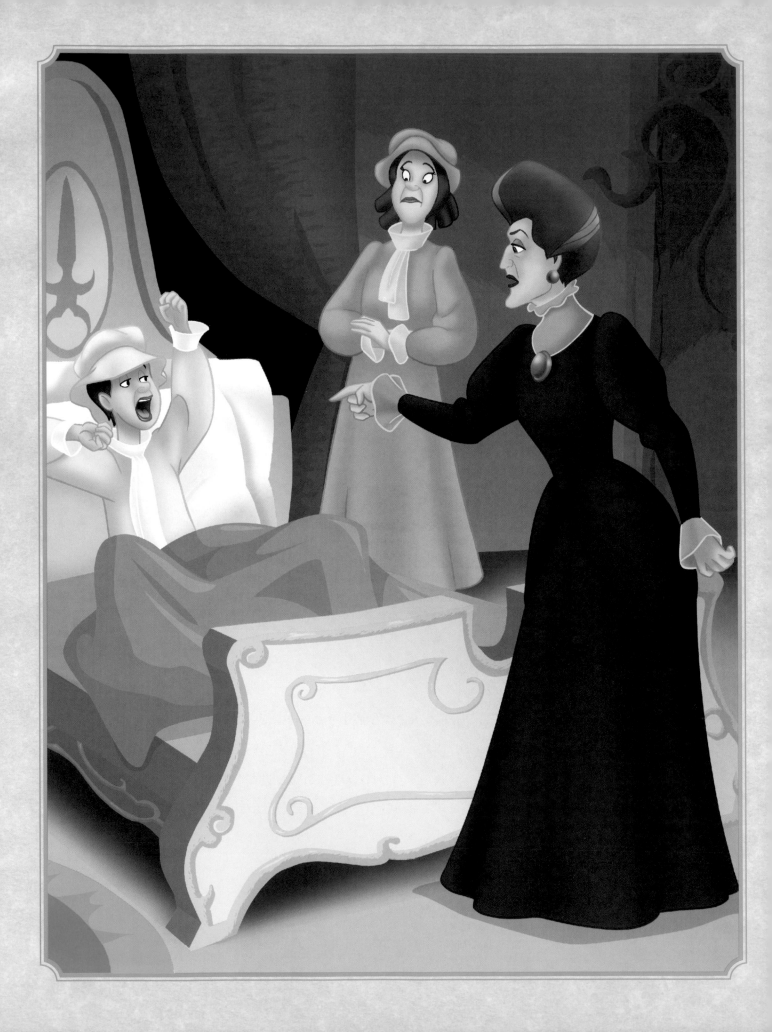

7

Mice Are Nice, Part 2

The next morning, I was surprised to find my entire stepfamily in Drizella's room. They were so agitated that they hardly noticed when I came in with the breakfast trays.

"Get up!" my stepmother was urging Drizella. "The Grand Duke will be here any minute. He's scouring the kingdom!"

Drizella's response was a bone-cracking yawn. "For what?" she asked sleepily.

"For a girl who dropped a glass slipper when she left the palace!" reported Anastasia. "The Prince is madly in love with her."

"So get out of bed and wash your feet!" shouted my stepmother. "If you or Anastasia can fit into the slipper, the Prince will marry you!"

I dropped the breakfast trays.

The handsome stranger with the SAVE THE WHALES pin—the man of my dreams—was the Prince! And he wanted to marry ME!

My stepmother told me to clean up the mess, but I was so giddy with happiness that I ignored her. Instead, I twirled out of the room, humming a waltz.

It was a bad mistake.

I was in my room, telling the mice the wonderful news about the Prince, when I recognized the heavy tread of my stepmother on the stairs. An instant later, she stood in the doorway of my little room.

"So, you like waltzes, do you? I thought I saw you at the ball," she hissed, drawing a big brass key out of her reticule. "You were there, monopolizing the prince! Keeping him from my daughters!"

"I was there," I admitted, "but I didn't know he—"

"Enough! I won't have you endangering the future of my girls! You're staying up here!" She slammed the door and locked me in.

"I can't believe she did that!" squeaked Gus, emerging from under my pillow. I sat down on the bed next to him.

"Believe it," said Jaq.

Gus jumped onto my lap. "Don't worry, Cinderella, we'll help you," he said. "We'll get the key."

"It's very sweet of you to offer," I said. "But that key is twice your size. It's much too heavy for you."

"We're stronger than we look," said Jaq as they left.

The next few minutes were long ones. I heard a carriage arrive and knew it must be the Grand Duke. I worried that Lucifer would harm Jaq and Gus. I wondered where my Fairy Godmother was, and if she handled escapes as well as makeovers.

Then I heard a thunk on the stairs.

I ran to the keyhole. Jaq and Gus were there—with the key!

"How did you *do* that?" I cried, after I had finally unlocked the door.

"Mice can carry fifty times their weight, remember?" said Jaq.

8

No Shoehorn Required

I raced downstairs.

A footman, carrying my glass slipper on a big velvet pillow, stood at the door as the Grand Duke made his farewells.

"Please!" I cried. "May I try on the slipper?" To my relief, the Duke was willing.

Unfortunately, my stepmother was not.

When the footman came toward me with the slipper, she stuck out her walking stick and tripped him. The slipper flew into the air, hit the floor, and shattered into a thousand pieces.

She could barely suppress a smile.

Anastasia and Drizella giggled.

The Grand Duke nearly wept. "This is terrible!" he cried. "The King will be furious! And the Prince will be so disappointed!"

I drew the other glass slipper out of my apron pocket. "Are you sure?" I asked, handing the slipper to him.

It fit me perfectly, of course.

The Grand Duke and I smiled at each other. It was a happy moment for both of us.

"You will have to do your own washing and ironing now," I told my stepfamily. "I'm going to be busy with other things."

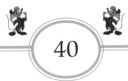

The Prince and I opened up our own practice as soon as we finished veterinary school. We're busy, but we love it. The mice and the horse and Bruno and the chickens live with us now, along with a host of other animals, and they're all very healthy. The guinea pigs have even agreed to be guinea pigs for my newest specialty—animal behavior modification.

I'm hoping to get Lucifer in for treatment.

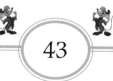

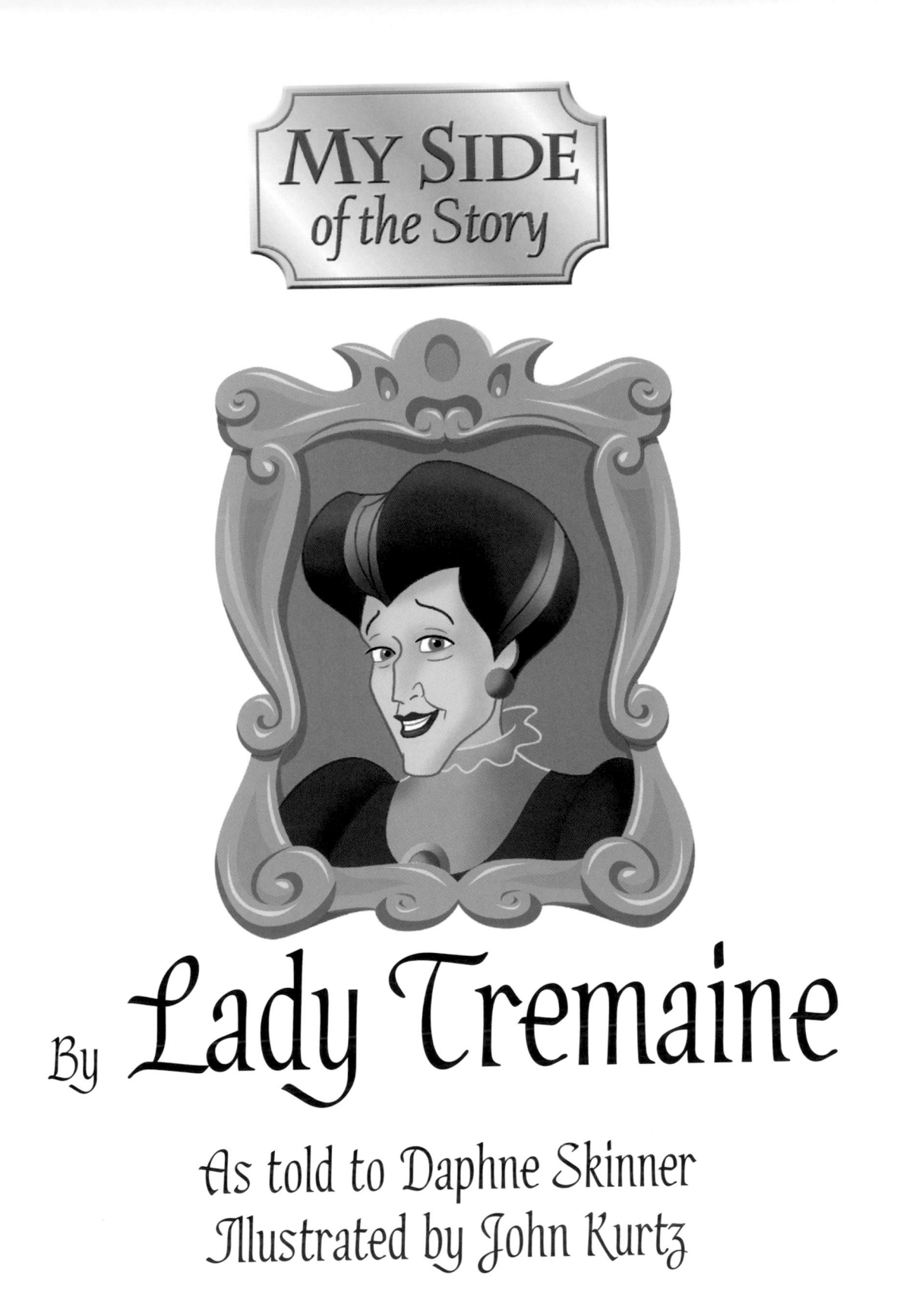

By Lady Tremaine

As told to Daphne Skinner
Illustrated by John Kurtz

1

Suspicion

J have always tried to do right by my daughters. Anastasia and Drizella are the sweetest, loveliest girls in the kingdom, and neither one of them would hurt a fly.

So, I feel I must tell the world about our relationship with their stepsister Cindy. Too many people believe that we mistreated Cindy, and were "cruel" to her. They've even accused us of making her a servant in her own house.

They are mistaken.

First, Anastasia and Drizella have always been delicate creatures, sensitive little things whose feelings bruised easily. When I married Cindy's father, they were as timid as mice. Cindy, on the other hand, was a rather odd, unruly little girl, always skipping off to the barnyard and talking to the animals. But she seemed good-natured, and I hoped she might befriend my darlings and help them to overcome their shyness.

I didn't know it then, but that was about as likely as a fox playing patty-cake with a pair of young rabbits.

I remember the day I first began to suspect that Cindy wasn't quite as sweet as she pretended to be. It was some time ago, during Signor Capezio's annual visit. He was fitting the girls for shoes, as he did every year.

He measured Anastasia and Drizella first. *"Madonna!"* he exclaimed. "I cannot believe it! You are both size ten! Last year, you were size seven!"

My daughters were eleven and twelve, and they had just gone through a dramatic growth spurt. They were very self-conscious about it, poor darlings. Anastasia had taken to dropping things and bumping into the furniture. Drizella bit her nails constantly.

"Mama?" croaked Anastasia. "Is that bad?"

"Are my feet too big?" quavered Drizella.

"Of course not!" I assured her. "Big feet are a sign of intelligence! Aren't they, Signore?"

But Signor Capezio didn't respond. He was busy measuring Cindy's feet. "Size four!" he gushed. "Not a millimeter more than last year. They are still *come fiorelli*—like little flowers!"

Cindy protested, as if his flattery embarrassed her. But I could sense her malicious glee.

And so could my girls.

A Major Change

J have strong maternal instincts, and when they warned me about Cindy, I listened. My girls had been hurt. I could see it in their downcast eyes, hear it in their quavering voices, and sense it in the way they slouched around in their bathrobes. I had to act quickly, before Cindy launched another sneak attack on their wobbly self-esteem.

So, the day after Signor Capezio's visit, I told my daughters that from then on they would be spending less time with their stepsister.

"You'll be too busy with your important new responsibilities," I explained. "From now on, you, Anastasia, will be in charge of coming to music lessons on time. You will also pick flowers for the luncheon table, and make sure your dirty clothing is in the laundry basket, where it belongs. And you, Drizella, will be in charge of wearing clean gloves to your dancing lessons. You will also decide which clothing has to be mended, and ring the dinner bell every evening."

My girls looked at me with dismay. It sounded like a lot of work, it's true. But I knew they were up to the challenge. There was a long silence while they thought this over. Then they asked, "Mama, what about Cindy? Does she have new responsibilities, too?"

"Yes, indeed," I replied. "Cindy will do the washing and the ironing," I said. "She will sweep and scrub and dust. She'll also serve us breakfast, do the mending, and feed the animals."

"That sounds fair," said Anastasia. Drizella nodded.

Tears filled my eyes. What good, brave girls I had!

3

Fair Is Fair

Years went by. Though Cindy had more work than ever (I saw to that), she was never too busy to connive against my girls. For example, she knew that Anastasia was terrified of mice. So, she cunningly hid a huge rodent under my poor daughter's teacup one morning. I have never heard such screams! They terrified me, and nearly sent Drizella into hysterics of her own.

Both girls were so shattered that I had to summon Monsieur Sédative, the nerve specialist, from France, and Herr Cerebrum, the analyst, from Austria. Even with the help of these renowned physicians, my darlings did not recover for days.

When they were finally well again, I gave them a music lesson. To my relief, Anastasia played beautifully, without once dropping her flute. Drizella sang like an angel, hitting at least every other note perfectly.

Then Cindy came into the music room, carrying a Royalgram. The King was giving a ball in honor of the Prince, and we were all invited! I was overjoyed, and so were my girls—until Cindy spoke up.

"The Royalgram says that all the eligible girls in the kingdom are invited," she said, fluffing her blond hair, batting her long eyelashes, and doing a pirouette on those tiny little feet. "I'm eligible. That means I'm invited, too."

Anastasia's flute clattered to the floor. Drizella's hands flew to her mouth, and she began chewing all ten fingernails at once.

My maternal instincts went on red alert, but what could I do? I had to be fair.

So I told the girls that as long as they finished their assigned tasks (and dressed themselves suitably), they could all go—even Cinderella.

Without another word, Anastasia hurried away to pick flowers and sort the laundry, and Drizella began deciding which clothes needed mending.

I was proud of them.

Happily, they soon finished these highly demanding tasks and spent the rest of the day preparing for the ball.

Cindy, on the other hand, took forever to accomplish her few simple chores (she spent hours cleaning the andirons, and even longer on the soup tureen), and by eight o'clock she hadn't finished polishing the fish knives.

Needless to say, she was still wearing her apron and kerchief.

We were ready by then, of course, and as it was rude to keep the coach waiting, we bid Cindy farewell. I should have known she would make a last-ditch effort to delay us, and she did. Just as we were walking out the door, she scrambled downstairs, wearing a hideous, ill-fitting frock that looked as if it had been sewn by rodents.

"Is there room for me in the coach?" she cried.

People have accused us of being unkind to Cindy, but I feel my daughters and I did her a great favor at that moment. We told her ever so gently that her dress was unsuitable and that she should stay at home.

It was our attempt to spare her a lifetime of embarrassment.

Shockingly, she was not the least bit grateful.

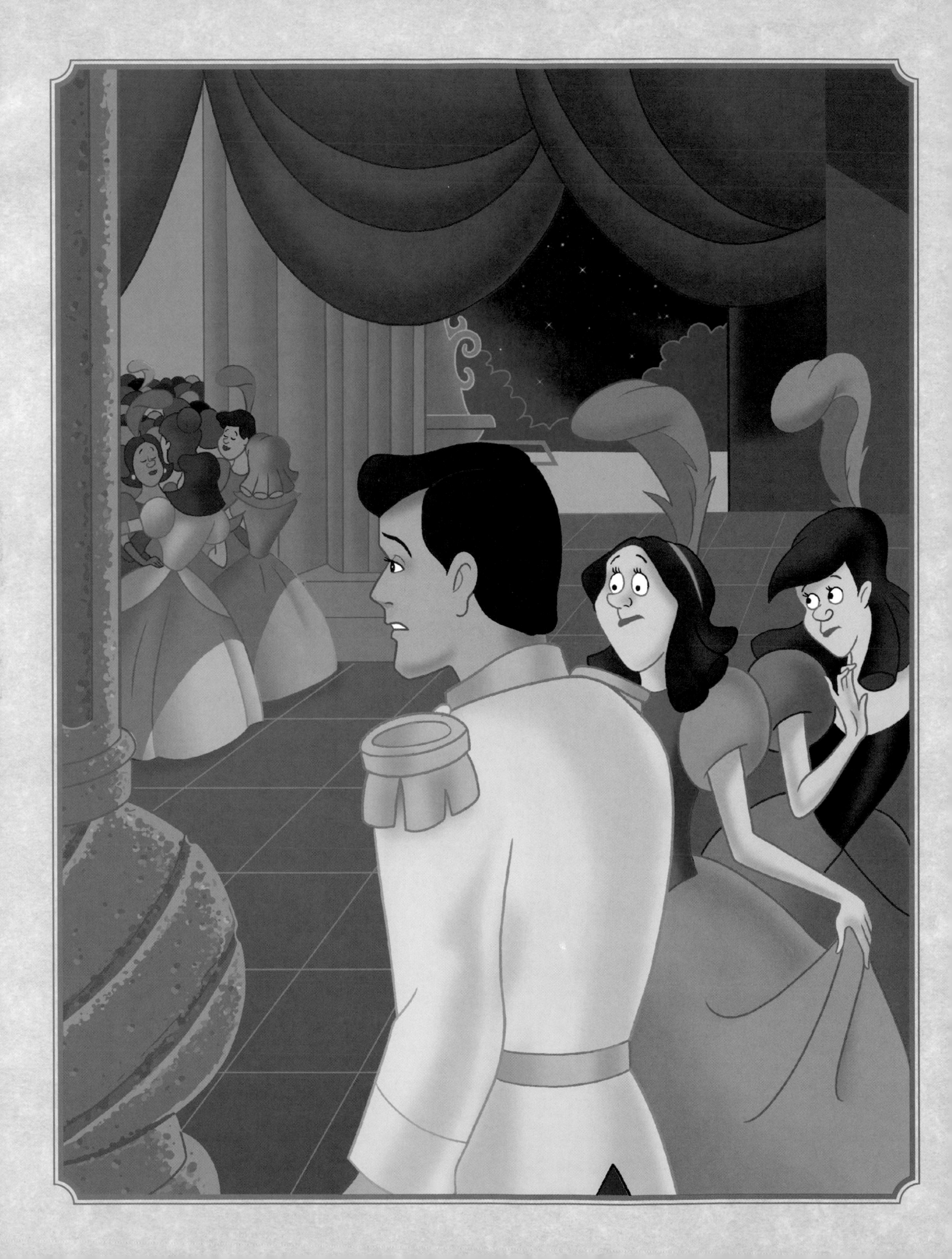

No Other Explanation

I would like to say that my girls met the Prince and charmed him off his feet, but, alas, that is not what happened. They met him, yes, and he was very polite, but when they tried to draw him out, he barely responded—his attention was clearly elsewhere. After a few distracted pleasantries, he excused himself and hurried away.

My girls were deeply disappointed. "Mama!" whimpered Drizella. "He hardly even talked to us!"

"And he never asked us to dance!" complained Anastasia.

"He hasn't asked anyone to dance," I pointed out, and it was true. The orchestra was playing, and the ballroom was full of beautifully dressed young ladies, but they were waltzing with one another.

The Prince was nowhere to be seen.

"I must get to the bottom of this," I thought, so I hurried to the powder room, which was crowded with frustrated mothers. Not surprisingly, the main topic of conversation was the Prince's odd behavior.

Then another mother entered, with the news that the Prince was in the garden—waltzing with a young woman!

"Who is she?" everyone asked in a chorus.

"I have no idea," replied the irate mother. "She must be a foreigner. Perhaps she's American."

What followed was disgraceful. Before I could make my way to the garden, I was pushed aside—no, trampled—by a violent stampede of ruthless matrons.

So, I did not get a good look at the mystery woman; I merely glimpsed her through the surging crowd. There was something strangely familiar about her, I thought.

Nevertheless, I had other things on my mind. The ball had been a big disappointment to my girls. Would they take it in stride, or start wandering around in their bathrobes again? I couldn't say.

Signor Capezio came bright and early the next morning to deliver my daughters' shoes—and to gossip about the ball.

"I heard *Il Principe* fell in love last night," he said, "with a petite, golden-haired beauty."

The one who was waltzing with him in the garden! I thought.

"It's incredible," he went on, "but this young lady—she wore slippers made of glass! In all my years as a shoemaker, I have never heard of such a thing! Ostrich leather, yes. Sharkskin, yes. But glass—no!" He shook his head in amazement.

"I heard also," he continued, "that she fled the palace at midnight, leaving one of her slippers behind. *Eccolo! Il Principe* wants to find her and marry her."

"That should be easy enough," I said. "He must have her address."

"No. He has only the glass slipper," replied Signor Capezio. "He says that the woman who fits it will be his bride. Even now, the Grand Duke is searching the kingdom. I passed him. He is coming this way."

"Are you saying that the Prince will marry any woman who can get her foot into the glass slipper?" I asked, and he nodded.

Then my girls still have a chance! I thought. Surely one of them can fit her foot into it! "Let me show you out, Signore," I said, leading him into the foyer.

"One other thing," he said, as I opened the door. "The slipper of glass? It is said to be very, very small." He bowed. *"Arrivederci, Signora."*

In my desperate haste to get my girls out of bed, I scarcely noticed Cindy. If she hadn't dropped the breakfast trays, I probably wouldn't have seen her at all.

But she did drop them—just as I was telling Drizella about the Prince's search for the mystery girl, and begging her to wash her feet before the Grand Duke arrived.

The crash startled me, but what startled me even more was Cindy's response when I asked her to clean up the mess. She ignored me! Then she pirouetted out the door, humming a waltz!

It was the very same waltz that had been playing at the ball! At that exact moment, my suspicions about my stepdaughter changed—for the worse. Obviously, Cinderella had gone to the ball. But how?

I racked my brains.

It finally came to me.

I do not like to use the words "black magic," but in this instance, I simply must—BLACK MAGIC! Cindy had used dark, magical powers to transform herself into a lady, go to the ball, and put a spell on the Prince!

When I thought of what she was capable of doing next, my blood ran cold.

When Bad Things Happen to Good Daughters

J have many regrets about that day. I shouldn't have locked Cindy in her room. I should have packed her straight off to Herr Cerebrum's Home for the Mentally Troubled. A few years of rest behind those tall barred windows might have done her some good—and saved my daughters the humiliation that followed.

As it was, Cindy quickly used her magic powers to free herself. She flounced downstairs before the Duke could leave—neither Anastasia nor Drizella had been able to fit into the glass slipper, though they had tried their little hearts out—and he was about to go.

The events of the next few moments are a blur. I remember Cindy fluttering her eyelashes at the Duke and extending her foot. I remember Anastasia's throaty cry of rage. I remember that Drizella began to hyperventilate. I may have tried to restrain them with my walking stick—I'm not sure.

I do know that in the confusion, the glass slipper flew into the air before it reached Cindy's foot, hit the floor, and broke into a thousand tiny pieces.

My girls and I froze. The Grand Duke wept.

Cinderella smiled. Then, *as if by magic*, she produced another glass slipper.

Of course, it fit her perfectly—that's what black magic is all about!

6

The Upside

Yesterday, as we were having tea, Anastasia started complaining. She does this often. "Cindy married the Prince," she moaned, with her mouth full of crumpet, "and we didn't!"

Before I could remind her not to talk with her mouth full, Drizella chimed in. "It isn't fair!" she whined.

"Girls!" I told them. "Count your blessings! We're all healthy. We're all together. There are no more mice in the house. And we even have a new servant." I rang the bell for Rumpelstiltskin, who scuttled in with a platter of tea cakes.

As soon as he had hurried away, Anastasia muttered, "There's something weird about him."

"I know what you mean," said Drizella. "He's got a huge chip on his shoulder."

"He's fast and efficient, and he keeps to himself," I said. "We're lucky to have him." Besides, I thought, he'll never cast a spell on us—like someone I could mention. So what if I have to pay him? At least I don't have to worry anymore.

And that's a real blessing.